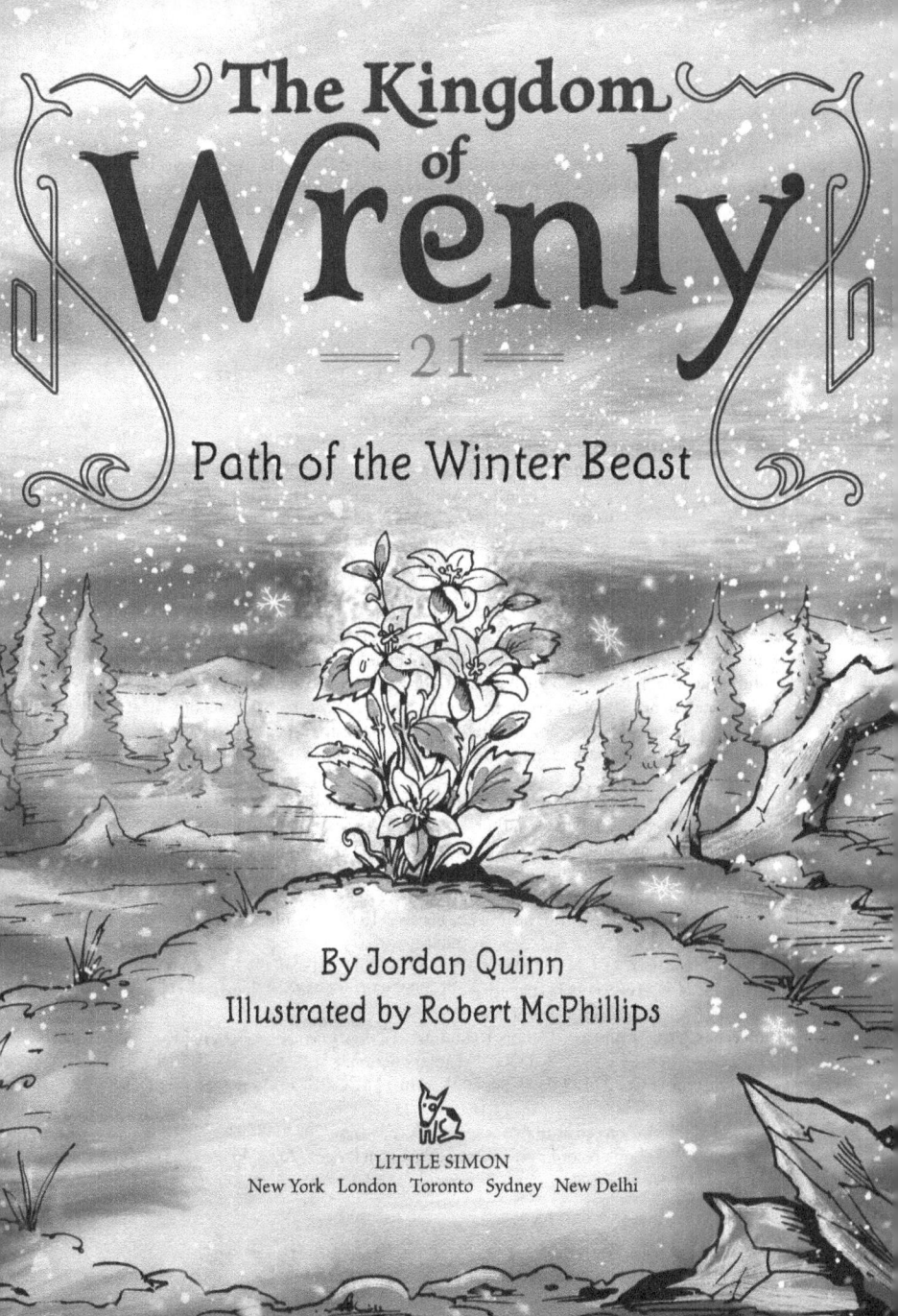

The Kingdom of Wrenly

21

Path of the Winter Beast

By Jordan Quinn
Illustrated by Robert McPhillips

LITTLE SIMON
New York London Toronto Sydney New Delhi

This book is a work of fiction. Any references to historical events, real people, or real places are used fictitiously. Other names, characters, places, and events are products of the author's imagination, and any resemblance to actual events or places or persons, living or dead, is entirely coincidental.

LITTLE SIMON
An imprint of Simon & Schuster Children's Publishing Division
1230 Avenue of the Americas, New York, New York 10020
First Little Simon edition August 2024
Copyright © 2024 by Simon & Schuster, LLC
All rights reserved, including the right of reproduction in whole or in part in any form.
LITTLE SIMON is a registered trademark of Simon & Schuster, LLC, and associated colophon is a trademark of Simon & Schuster, LLC.
Simon & Schuster: Celebrating 100 Years of Publishing in 2024
For information about special discounts for bulk purchases, please contact Simon & Schuster Special Sales at 1-866-506-1949 or business@simonandschuster.com.
The Simon & Schuster Speakers Bureau can bring authors to your live event. For more information or to book an event contact the Simon & Schuster Speakers Bureau at 1-866-248-3049 or visit our website at www.simonspeakers.com.
Manufactured in the United States of America 0724 LAK
2 4 6 8 10 9 7 5 3 1
Library of Congress Cataloging-in-Publication Data
Names: Quinn, Jordan, author. | McPhillips, Robert, 1971– illustrator.
Title: Path of the winter beast / by Jordan Quinn ; illustrated by Robert McPhillips.
Description: First Little Simon paperback edition. | New York : Little Simon, 2024. | Series: Path of the winter beast ; book 21 | Audience: Ages 5–9. | Summary: "Prince Lucas and Lady Clara venture into the heart of Flatfrost to face a winter beast"—Provided by publisher.
Identifiers: LCCN 2023048493 (print) | LCCN 2023048494 (ebook) | ISBN 9781665948432 (paperback) | ISBN 9781665948449 (hardcover) | ISBN 9781665948456 (ebook)
Subjects: CYAC: Animals—Fiction. | Tundras—Fiction. | Princes—Fiction. | Fantasy. | LCGFT: Fantasy fiction.
Classification: LCC PZ7.Q31945 Pat 2024 (print) | LCC PZ7.Q31945 (ebook) | DDC [Fic]—dc23
LC record available at https://lccn.loc.gov/2023048493
LC ebook record available at https://lccn.loc.gov/2023048494

CONTENTS

Chapter 1: An Ice-Cold Boom	1
Chapter 2: Prince Sleepyhead	11
Chapter 3: The Beast Catcher	21
Chapter 4: Half a Story	35
Chapter 5: Beast-Bound	45
Chapter 6: Liar, Liar	61
Chapter 7: It's *Snow* Laughing Matter!	71
Chapter 8: The Tale of Wynn	81
Chapter 9: We Have a Dragon	91
Chapter 10: The Protectors	107

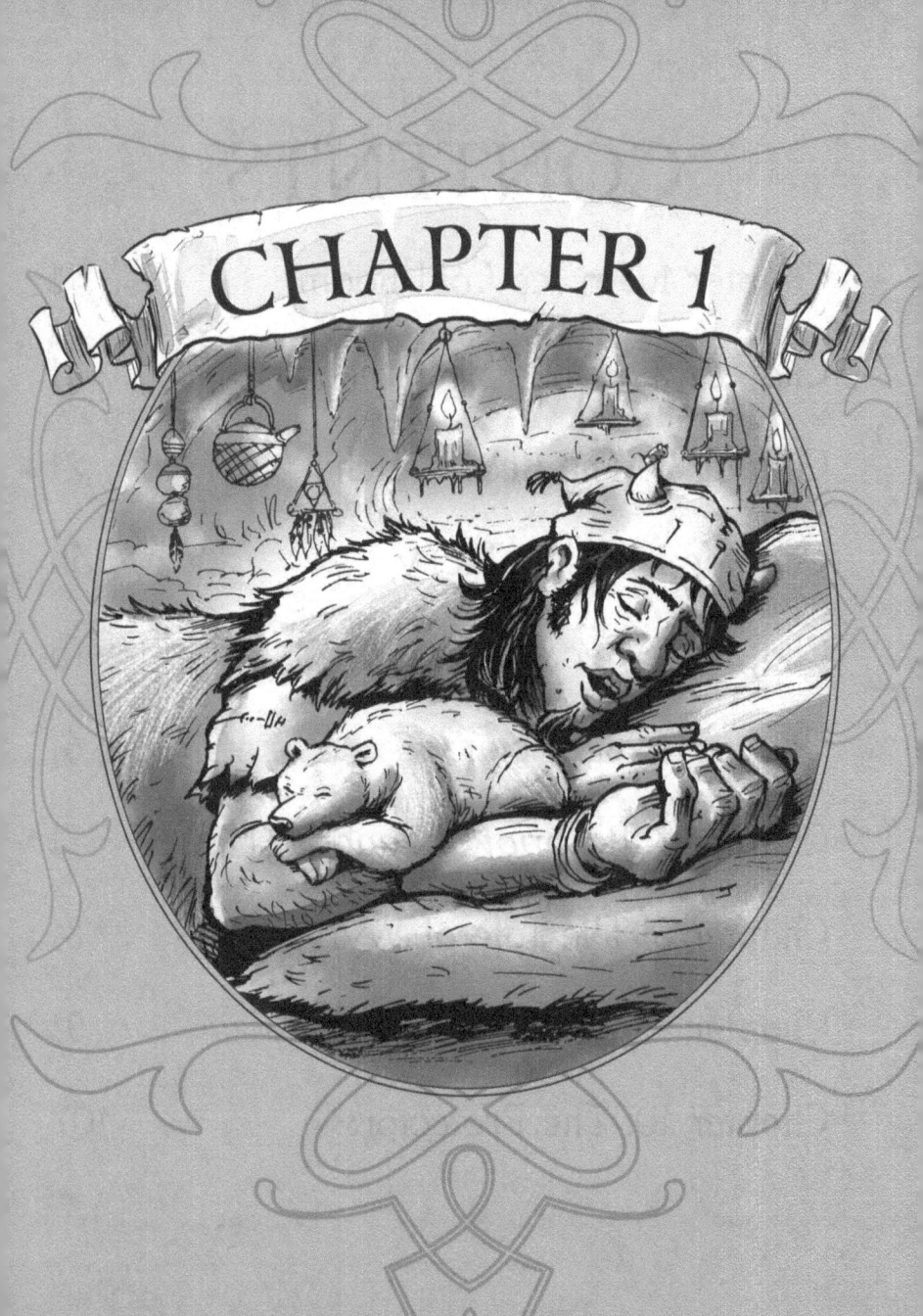

An Ice-Cold Boom

In Flatfrost, the land of the giants, it's winter year-round.

The trees are frozen over, icicles growing on their branches. The ground is packed with layers of snow. And in the middle of the night, everything sleeps deeply.

Gumlock, chief of the giants, was in one of these heavy slumbers. Nothing could possibly wake him.

Snow blanketed his cave, and all was quiet. The moonlight that streamed in only made it a cozier sight.

Nothing, not a single thing, could wake him. Not even—

Boom! Boom! Boom!

Suddenly, in the middle of his dreams, Gumlock heard the sound of thunder. It became louder and louder.

Boom! Boom! Boom!

The chief of the giants sat up in bed, startled out of his sleep. He looked around his home and saw nothing out of place.

"That thunder sounds terribly real," he said with a great yawn. "But I'm sure it's nothing to worry about."

He tried settling back to sleep, but the sound came again.

Boom! Boom! Boom!

It is real, he realized.

Leaping out of bed, Gumlock slipped on his boots and raced to the mouth of the cave.

Boom! Boom! Boom!

Gumlock gazed out into the night. A shadow cast itself across the moonlit snow. The giant stepped

out of the cave and gasped.

There in the moonlight was a beast larger than even a giant! Curling horns stretched from its head, and it had thick, shaggy fur. It stopped in its tracks and wailed mournfully into the dark night.

This creature . . . it looks familiar, Gumlock thought.

He watched as it let out another cry, then disappeared into the snowy wind.

Gumlock ran back into his cave. Before he faced the creature, he

needed to know more about it.

He went straight to his bookshelf and pulled out a book of ancient myths and legends. Gumlock flipped through the pages until he came to the one he was looking for. There, sketched perfectly, was the very same beast he'd just seen outside.

Wynnter Beast, the caption read.

WYNNTER BEAST

"It can't be!" he exclaimed.

Without wasting another second, Gumlock slammed the book shut, pulled on his coat, and rushed outside.

I must speak to the king right away! he thought.

CHAPTER 2

Prince Sleepyhead

Yawn . . . yawn . . . double yawn.

During his early morning history lesson, Prince Lucas could barely stay focused. Lady Winifred, his tutor, was reading him a story about an old legend. But all he could think about was the upcoming Winter Drop Festival.

His eyelids became heavy as he daydreamed about festival sweets.

Every few years the king and queen hosted a special festival in honor of the rare Winter Drop flower that grew in Flatfrost. The nectar of this star-shaped flower was the star of many baked goods. Everyone in the kingdom looked forward to the treats, but no one was more excited than Prince Lucas himself.

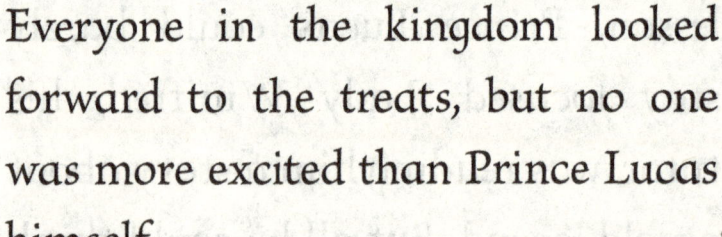

The flower only grew from the snow at random times, sometimes with many years in between. Finally, this year, the giants had reported seeing a batch sprouting. In no time their good friend Gumlock would bring the harvest!

Lady Winifred suddenly cleared her throat. "Are you even listening, Prince Lucas?" she asked. "What I'm reading is very important, you know."

Lucas sat up straight, rubbing his eyes. "Of course! I've heard every word!"

Lady Winifred smiled. She knew he hadn't been listening.

He smiled sheepishly. "Okay, maybe I should have paid closer attention."

The tutor closed her book.

"Your Highness, I chose this tale because I thought you'd like it,"

she said. "It's about the discovery of the Winter Drop flower."

"Oh, please read it again!" he begged. "I promise to listen this time."

Lady Winifred smiled. "We'll pick back up on it next time. We're

BRAVE WIZARD.

just getting to the good part, where a wizard saves the flowers from a wicked creature who wants to destroy them."

"Wow!" Lucas exclaimed. "It's been a while since I've heard a wizard story."

"Yes, and—" Lady Winifred was suddenly interrupted by the sound of guards rushing past the library.

Lucas turned to look. He caught a glimpse of a man wearing a fur cape and a large hat.

"This way, sir. Straight ahead to the king!" a guard shouted.

"Who is that?" Lucas wondered aloud, standing in order to see better.

Lady Winifred sighed.

"Oh, go on," she said. "See what the excitement is all about."

"Thanks, Lady Winifred!" Lucas said, racing into the hallway. "I promise to pay attention next time!"

The Beast Catcher

Clara Gills, the prince's best friend, arrived at the palace with a basket of freshly baked goods. There were butter rolls, almond cakes, and the king's favorite cinnamon bread.

Recognizing her, the guards bowed as she made her way to the entrance doors.

"Good day, Lady Clara," they both said.

She removed the cloth covering from the basket. "Care to try a roll? My father has baked them for the festival! All we're missing is the Winter Drop flower's syrup for an extra-sweet touch."

"We can't say no to that," one of the guards cheerfully replied.

They each took a bread roll, bit into it, and sighed happily.

"Perfect for the festival, don't you think?" Clara asked.

They nodded eagerly. She skipped onward, heading toward the throne room. Just as she was about to step in, the sound of bustling feet made Clara stop in her tracks.

Whoosh!

A group of guards rushed by her.

The cloth over her baked goods flew away.

"Move aside!" sneered a man with a cape.

Clara pulled her basket close. *Well, that was rude,* she thought. *Who is that?*

As the man in the cape and the guards swished into the throne room, the doors shut firmly behind them.

"That's one way to say that now's not a good time," she muttered.

"Clara!" someone called. "I'm so glad you're here!"

She turned around and saw the prince hurrying toward her. "Lucas!"

Lucas stopped and pointed at her basket. "I hope these are *all* for me."

"I suppose someone's got to eat them." Clara offered Lucas the basket.

He helped himself to an almond cake and ate it hungrily. Crumbs flurried to the floor.

Clara laughed. "Hungry much?"

Lucas blushed. "Everyone needs a snack before a new adventure."

"Does this adventure involve a rude man in a cape and a giant hat?" Clara asked.

Lucas took another roll and nodded. "How did you know?"

"He's in there, speaking to your parents." Clara jerked her thumb toward the shut doors.

"It's a good thing I'm the prince!" Lucas replied. "I can get us in. Coming?"

"I've finished all my chores for today, so . . ." Clara shrugged. "I'm up for it."

She followed Lucas. Very slowly, he pushed open the heavy doors. When there was just enough space for them both, they slid in and hid behind a pillar.

"Whoa," Lucas whispered. "Look at all the guards."

Whatever is happening seems important, Clara thought.

The man with the cape stood before the king and queen.

"Your Majesties!" he said dramatically, without bowing. "Thank you for honoring my request to see you. Allow me to introduce myself. I'm Lord Mal, the Beast Catcher, and I've come from far away to help solve your rather *large* problem."

"Problem?" Lucas whispered. "What problem?"

On his throne King Caleb raised an eyebrow. "I see that word travels fast. You must be here because the Winter Drop flower harvest is gone."

Clara covered her mouth as she gasped.

CHAPTER 4

Half a Story

Lucas couldn't believe what he'd just heard. The Winter Drop harvest was . . . gone?

"We thank you for coming, Lord Mal," Queen Tasha said. "Could you tell us a bit about yourself?"

"Why, I am known for my excellent work of catching the most terrible creatures across all the land," the Beast Catcher said smugly.

"Is that so?" King Caleb asked.

"Have no fear—I'll find this Flatfrost beast and make it disappear as if by magic," said Lord Mal.

Clara whispered, "Have you ever heard of a Flatfrost beast?"

Lucas shook his head. "Nope."

There were giants in Flatfrost, but they were friendly.

"What do we know of this creature?" King Caleb asked. "Surely it must have its reasons for taking the harvest."

Lord Mal frowned. "It is a monster, Your Majesty. All monsters are evil."

A giant shadow cast itself across the throne room. Lucas looked up to see Gumlock the giant looking in through a throne room window. Clara and Lucas waved eagerly but then dropped their hands. Their friend looked gloomy.

"May I say something?" Gumlock asked through the window.

King Caleb nodded. "Please speak, friend. You did warn us about this beast early in the morning, after all."

The giant bowed his head. "I, too, am worried about the

Winter Drop harvest disappearing. But unlike Lord Mal, I do not think this creature is evil. I think it is . . . afraid."

Everyone in the room began to whisper and exchange looks of disbelief.

The king raised his hand. The room became silent.

"Afraid?" Lord Mal laughed rudely. "Do you hear yourself? The beast is wicked! It must be caught immediately."

King Caleb said, "I'm sorry, Gumlock. We cannot risk having a dangerous beast running free. It's for the good of Wrenly."

Gumlock nodded sadly and turned to leave.

"You may do your job," Queen Tasha said to Lord Mal. "But, please, be as gentle as you can. We know nothing about the beast or its true reasons for taking the flowers."

"Of course." Lord Mal bowed fully this time. Even with his face so low to the ground, his smile was unkind. "I'll be as gentle as I know how to be."

Clara squeezed Lucas's arm. "I don't know about you, but I think there's more to this story than what we're hearing."

The prince nodded. "We need to find out what's *really* going on."

Beast-Bound

Lucas and Clara raced up the spiral stone steps to the prince's bedroom. If they were going to Flatfrost, they would need the right clothing to keep warm.

They burst into the room. From his fluffy bed, the prince's scarlet dragon lifted his head curiously.

"We're going on a frosty mission, Ruskin!" Lucas said.

Ruskin squawked and flapped his wings in approval.

Clara tossed Ruskin the last roll remaining in her basket. As it flew through the air, Ruskin set it ablaze and swallowed the perfectly toasted treat.

Meanwhile, Lucas pulled out winter clothes from a wooden chest. Hats, gloves, scarves, sweaters, and coats piled near Clara.

She grabbed a jacket and slipped it on. "Perfect!"

"Make sure to grab gloves and a warm cap, too," Lucas said, slipping on his attire. "We've got to hurry. If we catch Gumlock before he leaves the castle grounds, we can ride with him to Flatfrost."

"Good thinking," Clara said.

In a hurry the friends raced down the castle stairs and outside. But their giant friend was nowhere in sight.

"Oh no!" Lucas groaned. "What if he's already left?"

Neigh!

A large purple-and-gold carriage pulled into view. It was so large, it needed six horses to pull it.

"Well . . . *he's* still here," Clara grumbled.

Lord Mal, the Beast Catcher, stomped with his gold-buckled boots toward the fancy carriage. One of his personal guards, also wearing purple, opened the door for him.

"I can't believe I'm saying this," Lucas said, "but I think he's our fastest way to Flatfrost."

Clara groaned. "At least we can try to find out more about him. Ruskin, you'll keep an eye out, won't you?"

With a nod, Ruskin shot up into the air. Lucas knew he'd be watchful from above.

The prince turned toward the carriage. "Here goes nothing. . . ."

Together they walked up to the grumbling Beast Catcher.

"Excuse me, Lord Mal?" Lucas called.

"What do you want?" The man

turned and narrowed his eyes.

He doesn't know who Lucas is, Clara realized. *He doesn't even know he's speaking to Wrenly royalty!*

This might help them be sneaky. She smiled broadly. "Oh, we're big fans of yours! It would be our honor

to join you on your dangerous quest."

Lord Mal barked out a laugh. "What nonsense! Children do not go on quests."

We've gone on plenty of quests, Clara wanted to say.

Thinking fast, Lucas lifted Lord Mal's cape as he climbed into his carriage. The man turned around, surprised by the help.

Clara smiled. "See? We'll even carry your cape so it doesn't drag in the snow."

"It's a very fancy cape," Lucas added. "I bet not even the prince has something this . . . this . . . uh, expensive?"

Clara tried not to laugh.

The Beast Catcher sighed. "This cape *is* very expensive, and I would prefer it didn't get wet."

He glared at the kids. "Very well. You may join me. But hurry! You're keeping me from the king's payment—I mean, from saving the kingdom!"

Lord Mal stepped into his carriage with lots of fuss. Lucas and Clara followed, sitting across from him on purple velvet seats.

The driver slapped the reins, and the carriage rattled across cobblestones. Clara gazed out the window and saw Ruskin following at a safe distance.

That had been surprisingly easy. Now they were beastward-bound!

Liar, Liar

Lord Mal dressed richly, and he used perfume richly too. He took out a purple bottle and sprayed, sprayed, and sprayed. Lucas and Clara tried their best not to sneeze at the strong, too-sweet scent.

Lord Mal also liked staring at his fancy rings . . . a lot.

"So . . . have you always lived in Wrenly?" Clara asked.

Lord Mal admired himself in the window. "Are you speaking to *me*?"

"I am!" she said. "As we *said*, we're big fans of yours—right, *Luke*?"

Lucas nodded. He was thankful

Clara hadn't used his real name. If Lord Mal knew he was the king's son, would he act differently?

"That's right!" Lucas said. "We're so impressed by your many, um, beastly victories and your fancy stuff."

Lord Mal twisted a corner of his mustache. "I *am* very impressive," he bragged. "Why, everyone has given me so much gold for helping them that I own more castles than the king of Wrenly himself!"

If he has so much gold already, then why is he working to catch this beast? Lucas wondered.

"Has this always been your job?" asked the prince.

"Goodness no!" Lord Mal sneered. Then he quickly added, "Well, I mean, not always. It's a more recent hobby, though I've always been good at capturing things, no matter how dangerous."

Clara gently nudged Lucas's elbow. Lucas did the same thing back. They both agreed on one thing: Lord Mal was a total liar.

The carriage clattered on.

Outside, the world was getting frostier. Soon the carriage stopped. The kids peered out at the snowy landscape and snow-frosted pine trees. They had arrived in Flatfrost.

One of the guards opened the door of the carriage.

"Make sure that my expensive cape doesn't touch the ground!" commanded Lord Mal as he stood.

The kids lifted the back of the Beast Catcher's cape and held it up.

Outside, there was nothing unusual . . . at first. Then Lucas gasped as he noticed giant footsteps heading into the trees.

"Aha," Lord Mal said with a smile. "Follow the tracks in the snow! We have a beast to catch."

It's *Snow* Laughing Matter!

The bitter wind caught the Beast Catcher's cape, and it filled like a sail. Lucas and Clara held it in place as they trudged along behind him.

"We have to sneak away," Clara whispered to Lucas. "Gumlock's cave isn't too far from here."

The prince nodded. "I know, but how are we going to get away from all these guards?"

Clara grinned like a fox. "All we have to do is act like kids! Here, hold my side of the cape."

Lucas grabbed both sides of Lord Mal's cape and kept walking. Clara stooped down in the snow and formed a snowball. Then she hurled it.

Splat! It hit Lord Mal in the hat, which went crooked.

"GAH!" he cried, whirling around.

Lucas and Clara laughed.

"Snowball fight!" cried Clara.

Snowballs began to fly. Even the guards got into it. But not for long.

"STOP THIS AT ONCE!" Lord Mal bellowed, ducking from a soaring snowball.

Clara lay down on the snow. "Now let's make *snow angels*!"

She swished her arms and legs

back and forth in the snow.

Lucas dropped onto the snow and did the same.

"STOP THIS CHILDISH NONSENSE!" the Beast Catcher shouted. "Aren't you listening to me? Stop this!"

Lucas sat up, slumping dramatically as if he were too tired to stand. "You go ahead, sir. We'll catch up as soon as we're done playing in the snow."

Lord Mal brushed the snow off his cape. "Good riddance! And if you get lost, it's *not* my problem!"

The Beast Catcher snapped his fingers, and he and his guards marched on toward the forest.

The prince tossed a snowball at Clara, and it bounced off her back.

"Nice going!" Clara said, laughing as they hurried toward Gumlock's cave.

The giant was shoveling snow when they arrived. To their surprise, Gumlock looked as if he'd been expecting them.

"Ah, there you are," he said with a kind smile. "I knew it wouldn't take you long to follow."

"How did you know we'd come?" Clara asked.

"Heroes never take long before coming to help others," Gumlock said wisely. "Now come along as I tell you a story of long, long ago...."

CHAPTER 8

The Tale of Wynn

Clara and Lucas followed Gumlock into the wintry trees and listened to the giant's tale.

"Long ago," he began, "before Wrenly was a kingdom, we giants already lived here in Flatfrost. In those days there lived a giant named Wynn. He cared for the forest. And one wintry day, like this one, Wynn discovered the first Winter Drop flower. He nurtured it, and many grew."

"I didn't know so many things could grow in the snow," Lucas said, brushing his hand across plants

growing up from the ground.

"All things can grow," Gumlock said. "So long as they're cared for in the right manner."

He stopped to help Lucas and

Clara over a frozen creek. Then he continued his story.

"Wynn shared the beauty of the Winter Drop flower with everyone. Its syrupy taste was beloved, and word spread throughout other lands. Before long, a wizard arrived

and tried to destroy the flower."

"But why?" Clara cried.

"The wizard didn't like others having something that he couldn't have as well," Gumlock explained. "And outside of Flatfrost, the flower won't grow. But Wynn rose up against

him, forbidding him from taking the flower. And the wizard . . . well, he cursed Wynn to look like a beast."

Lucas couldn't believe what he was hearing. "This sounds just like what my tutor was trying to tell me this morning," he said. "Could Wynn be the beast Lord Mal is after? He's not just a character from a story?"

Gumlock nodded. "I'm sure of it."

Clara frowned. "What do you think made Wynn return now to take the harvest?"

"The only thing I can think of is that the wizard has returned too," Gumlock said. "And he's here to stop it from happening. The only problem is . . . no one knows what the wizard looks like."

"We've got an evil wizard *and* a beast catcher to worry about," Lucas grumbled. "Great."

They walked until the forest opened up into a vast snowfield.

"This is the secret location of the Winter Drops," said Gumlock. "Well, it *was* a secret."

Lucas and Clara looked around. There wasn't a single Winter Drop bud to be seen. The snow was tossed about, as if everything had been dug up from it.

A glint in all the whiteness caught Clara's eye. She stooped down and dug out an ice-blue flower.

"Wynn must've missed *this* one!" she gasped.

It was the only remaining Winter Drop.

We Have a Dragon

Clara gently lifted the Winter Drop flower from the ground, roots and all. Its star-shaped petals twinkled in the sun. Beads of syrup formed on the petals.

She licked the syrup from her thumb. "Mmm, delicious!"

Lucas shook his head. "Why would Wynn take the flowers? What's he doing with them now?"

Gumlock kneeled beside Clara. "I think Wynn has hidden the flowers to protect them."

"Well, let's protect this one just in case," Lucas said.

Clara cupped her hand around the precious flower.

At the same time, a giant shadow covered them. The friends looked up into a pair of dark, icy cold eyes. A roar filled the air.

"Wynn!" whispered Gumlock.

Clara slowly stood up to talk to the beast. When the beast saw the Winter Drop flower in her hand, he

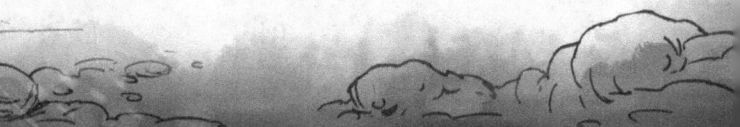

reached down and lifted both Clara and the flower up to his shaggy fur face.

Gumlock leaped to his feet.

"Wynn—is it you? Please, put her down," he said firmly. "Clara is a friend, not a foe."

Wynn's eyes were fixed on the Winter Drop flower in Clara's hand. Clara understood what Wynn was thinking.

"I'm not *taking* this flower," she assured him. "I only wanted to look at it. It belongs to Flatfrost."

Wynn's face softened, and he gently set Clara back on the ground.

Lucas wrapped his arms around his best friend. "Whew! Well done, Clara!"

And no sooner had they sighed with relief than they heard a terrible, evil laugh. It was Lord Mal and his army of guards!

"Yes, *well done*, children!" the Beast Catcher mocked. "And thank you for making my job so easy!"

"Wait," Lucas said. "This beast—his name is actually Wynn. He's not evil!"

But Lord Mal snapped his fingers. A guard loaded an arrow and released it.

Whoosh! The arrow whistled through the air. A net shot from the tip and wrapped around the beast. Wynn roared and staggered backward.

"Stop!" Gumlock cried. "You're making a grave mistake!"

Lord Mal ignored him, raising his hands. "Now let's make sure I don't make the same mistake as last time."

A crackle of ice burst from his hands, launching out toward Wynn. Ice covered the beast, freezing him in place. The guards, too, raised spears of what looked like icy magic.

The kids gasped.

"The spears are MAGIC!" Lucas cried. Then he spun around and faced Lord Mal. "You're *not* a beast

catcher. You're the evil wizard from long ago!"

Lord Mal laughed like a madman as the magical icy light surrounded the roaring beast. Ice began to form around Wynn's feet and slowly spread up his body. Gumlock ran to help, but Lord Mal made the magic capture him, too.

"The beast is MINE!" he cried. "Now to collect my gold! But first I need the Winter Drop flowers! I'll take those, too, and make a fortune selling them."

"If you take them out of Flatfrost, they won't ever grow again," warned Clara.

But Lord Mal just shrugged. "That's not my problem. Besides, who will stop me? You're just kids."

Lucas stepped forward. "That's where you're wrong. I am the prince of Wrenly."

"And we have a dragon," Clara finished with a smile.

Lucas folded his arms. "You'll never get away with this!"

ROAR!

On the word "dragon," Ruskin swooped onto the battlefield. A wave of fire gushed from his jaws, melting the ice surrounding Wynn.

The Beast Catcher shielded himself with his arms. "Guards! Stop him!" he shouted.

The Protectors

The guards aimed their magical spears at Ruskin. Bolts of sparkling electricity poured from their arrows.

Fizzzzz! Whizzzz! ZAP!

Ruskin spewed fire at the bolts of electric ice.

KABOOM!

The ice shattered into streaming fireworks. Gumlock summoned his strength and burst out of the ice.

Ruskin continued flying over the guards while spewing fire, melting their icy weapons.

"Run for cover!" one shouted, darting into the forest. The rest followed him into hiding.

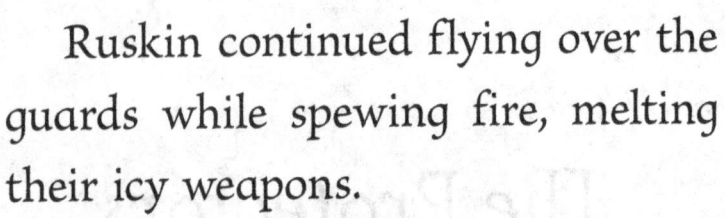

"Come back, you fools!" Lord Mal bellowed.

But none returned.

"Very well. I shall finish the job myself!" Lord Mal raised the only spear that hadn't melted. He pointed it at Wynn.

"No!" Lucas cried.

A howl rose from deep within Wynn. He charged at Lord Mal, knocking the magical spear from

the wizard's hand. It snapped into pieces.

Ruskin soared after him, helping scare away the evil wizard.

"*Yeooooow!*" shrieked the wizard as he fell to the ground. "Please! I was only trying to help your beloved kingdom of Wrenly!"

Lucas, Clara, and Ruskin approached the fallen wizard. Wynn and Gumlock stood behind them protectively.

"You are no friend to Wrenly," the prince said. "And Wrenly is no friend to you."

Gumlock picked up Lord Mal by the back of his fur cape.

"You're the *real* beast," he said. "And before I take you to the king, I order you to remove the enchantment from Wynn once and for all."

Lord Mal knew he had no choice. He faced Wynn and chanted a spell.

*"Let the powers in me be unleashed.
With this spell, the giant is released.
Now he shall no longer be a beast!"*

A shimmering wind swirled around Wynn. It danced around him, then burst away. Where there had once been a beast, there was now a giant whose eyes shone with joy.

Wynn ran his hands down his arms, then felt his face.

"I'm free," he marveled. "I'm *finally* free!"

Lucas and Clara cheered.

Wynn bowed. "How can I ever thank you?"

Clara smiled. "Well… I can think of just one tiny way."

The Winter Drop Festival was the best in Wrenly's history.

King Caleb and Queen Tasha honored Wynn as their special guest. He was given a special golden pin, naming him a protector of Wrenly. Everyone welcomed him happily.

A new rule was decreed that the kingdom would be allowed one Winter Drop flower per year. Now that Lord Mal was no longer a threat, there was no reason for Wynn to try to hide them.

As the kingdom celebrated,

Clara and Lucas sat near the town square's fountain. Their fingers were sticky from the sweet cakes they'd eaten.

"Ah," Lucas breathed out happily. "What a perfect way to end this adventure."

"We also helped free Wynn from his curse," Clara pointed out.

Lucas smiled sheepishly. "That, too!"

Clara nodded. "And now that we're honorary protectors, we, too, have become part of the Tale of Wynn!"

"Next time my tutor tells the story," Lucas said, "she'll have to tell everyone our names as well."

They laughed and ate more sweets, not letting one single syrupy drop go to waste.